Mickey's Young Readers Library • Mickey's Young Readers Library • Mickey

Mickey's Young Readers Library • Mickey's Young Readers Library • Mickey's Young Readers I

Mickey's Young Readers Library • Mickey's Young Rea

This Book Belongs to:

Mickey's
Young Readers Library

VOLUME
13
Mickey's Little Helpers

STORY BY MARY CAREY

Activities by Thoburn Educational Enterprises, Inc.

A BANTAM BOOK
NEW YORK · TORONTO · LONDON · SYDNEY · AUCKLAND

Mickey's Little Helpers   A Bantam Book/September 1990. All rights reserved. © 1990 The Walt Disney Company. Developed by The Walt Disney Company in conjunction with Nancy Hall, Inc. This book may not be reproduced or transmitted in any form or by any means.
ISBN 0–553–05628–X
Published simultaneously in the United States and Canada. Bantam Books are published by Bantam Doubleday Dell Publishing Group, Inc. Its trademark, consisting of the words "Bantam Books" and the portrayal of a rooster, is Registered in U.S. Patent and Trademark Office and in other countries. Marca Registrada. Bantam Books 666 Fifth Avenue, New York, New York 10103.
Printed in the United States of America
0 9 8 7 6 5 4 3 2 1
A Walt Disney BOOK FOR YOUNG READERS

Mickey was very happy. He stared at the sign in the shop window, and he smiled a big smile.

"How about that?" he asked. "It took all my money. I even sold my car. But I have my own shop at last."

"It looks great, Uncle Mickey," said Morty.

"Sure does!" Ferdie nodded. "Now we're all ready. We just sit back and wait for the customers."

"Right," said Mickey, "but let's act busy while we wait."

Morty went into the shop and began to sweep the floor. Ferdie dusted the safety helmets. Mickey worked on an old bike frame.

Mickey and the boys worked and swept and dusted all that day. It didn't help. Not a single customer came to the shop.

"It's too soon," Mickey decided. "People don't know we're here yet. We'll have lots of customers once they find out."

"Sure, Uncle Mickey." Ferdie stopped dusting. "Soon they'll know about us, and we'll be real busy."

Morty stopped sweeping. He had spotted a shiny new ten-speed bike on the rack. "Uncle Mickey, could I ride that bike?" he asked. "Just for a while? Just until someone wants to buy it?"

Ferdie ran to the rack to pick out a bike.
"How about this one?" he asked. "Can I ride it for a while? It's a neat bike."

"It is a neat bike," said Mickey. "But remember, all the bikes in this shop are for sale. We can't use them as if they were toys."

The boys knew Mickey was right. They said no more about the bikes. But as days went by and no customers came to the shop, they began to worry. Mickey put an ad in the newspaper. No one came.

"Maybe no bike riders live near here," said Morty.

"There must be *some* bike riders," Mickey said. "Anyway, we've worked so hard to set up this shop, we can't give up yet."

More days went by, and the mail carrier brought
bills. But Mickey had no customers. How could he
pay bills?

"We have money, Uncle Mickey." Morty ran
and got his piggy bank. "There must be ten dollars
here. Maybe more. You can use it."

"Thanks," said Mickey, "but things aren't *that*
bad. Not yet, anyway."

"Things aren't that good," said Ferdie.

"I wish we knew an elf," said Morty. "He could whisper to bikers about the great bike shop we have."

Mickey smiled a small smile. Then he sighed a big sigh. "Great idea, but there are no such things as elves, or leprechauns. If we succeed, we do it on our own."

Just as Mickey said this, a man came into the shop. He wore a helmet, and he was wheeling a bike. "Hello there, I need some help," he said. "Can you put new brakes on my bike by six o'clock tomorrow?"

A customer! At last! "No problem," Mickey told the man. "The bike will be as good as new by tomorrow night."

"No, no!" said the man. "Not tomorrow night!
Tomorrow *morning!* Six tomorrow morning!"

Mickey looked at the clock. It was six o'clock
now—six o'clock in the evening. Tomorrow morning
was only 12 hours away.

"There's a bike race up Thunder Mountain
tomorrow," said the biker. "It starts at six-thirty in the
morning. What do you say? Can you get my bike
ready in time?"

Mickey thought for a whole minute. Then he
managed to smile again. "I can do it," he said.
"Great!" The customer took his pack and left.
"Uncle Mickey, can you really fix the brakes that
fast?" asked Ferdie.
Mickey nodded. "I can if I work all night. I'll
need to buy some parts before I start."

"Parts?" Now Morty looked worried. "Where will you get parts? It's so late. All the stores that sell bike parts are closed by now."

"Maybe not all of them," said Mickey. "Get the phone book. I'll call around."

The boys got the book and looked up numbers. Mickey dialed the phone and dialed the phone. At last he got an answer. It was a store in the city.

"I have the parts you need," said the man on the phone, "but we close at eight. You can pick them up if you get here before then."

"Fine," said Mickey. "I'm on my way."

Mickey hung up and began to look for money. He turned his pockets inside out. He looked high and low, all through the house.

"There!" he said, when he had found enough money.

He took his old bike from the rack. "Don't wait up for me," he said. "I'll be late." Then he set out to ride the long miles to the city.

The boys were in bed when Mickey got back with the parts. "I wish I were in bed, too," thought Mickey. "I'm tired from pedaling all that way."

But there was no time to sleep. Mickey went to his worktable. He started to fix the customer's bike. Soon he yawned. He closed his eyes. Then, without even knowing it, he was fast asleep.

The sun was bright when Mickey woke up. "Oh, no!" he cried. "It's morning! I didn't fix the bike. That customer will be so angry."

Then Mickey saw the bike. It *was* fixed. It was as good as new.

Morty and Ferdie came out of their room.

"Look," cried Mickey. "The bike is fixed, but I didn't fix it!"

"You mean someone helped you?" asked Morty.

"Maybe it was elves!" added Ferdie.

The customer came to the door just then, and Ferdie ran to let him in. When he saw his bike, he smiled.

"Looks great!" he said. "And just in time for the Thunder Mountain race. I'm going to tell the other bike riders about your fast service!"

That day a lot of customers came to Mickey's shop.

"There's going to be a second bike race tomorrow," said the bike riders. "We'll need our bikes by morning."

"You'll have them by morning," Mickey said.

That night Mickey needed to buy parts again. This time he didn't have to turn out his pockets or look high and low through the house for money. He could buy the parts with the money the first biker had paid him.

Again Mickey got ready. Again he took his bike and rode away to the city.

Mickey got back after midnight, more sleepy
than ever. He set to work. And again he fell asleep.

Morty and Ferdie peeked out from the back of
the shop.

"It's okay," whispered Morty. "He's asleep."

Carefully, quietly, Morty and Ferdie began to fix
the bikes.

Mickey slept on.

Or did Mickey really sleep? Once Morty looked around and thought Mickey's eyes were open. He looked again quickly. "No," he whispered. "It's okay. He's still sleeping."

When Mickey woke in the morning, the bikes were ready. Mickey smiled. "I sure am lucky to have a couple of elves helping me," he said.

Mickey went to wake the boys. It wasn't easy. "Come on!" He shook Morty. "Out of bed. Time for school!"

Morty sat up at last. He was still sleepy—as sleepy as if he had been up all night. "Did you fix all the bikes?" Morty asked.

"They're fixed, but I didn't do it," Mickey told him. "The elves must have come back again."

Ferdie rubbed his eyes. "You said there weren't any such things as elves," he said. "Hey, maybe grownups don't know everything."

When the customers came for their bikes, everything was ready. The bikers promised to tell everyone in their biking club about Mickey's super service.

"I'll pass the word to other clubs, too," said one man. "Soon everyone will know about your bike shop."

The next day, Mickey's shop was crowded. It was crowded the day after that, and every day after that, too. Bike riders went out of their way to stop at Mickey's Bike Shop.

Mickey sold new helmets. He sold jackets. When he was not selling things, he was fixing things.

"I'm glad these aren't all rush orders," he said.

"So are we," the boys agreed.

One day soon after that, the boys got home
from school and saw two empty spaces on the rack.
"Oh, Uncle Mickey!" cried Ferdie. "You sold
those bikes we like."
"Sorry, boys," said Mickey. "I had to sell them.
That's why we opened the shop—to sell things."
"I guess so," sighed Morty.
Ferdie didn't say anything, but he looked sad.

Mickey hurried off to fix dinner.
"Say, what smells so great?" asked Ferdie.
"I'm making a fancy dinner," Mickey said.
"We've earned it. Later, I'll reward those elves who keep helping us out whenever we need it."
    "Reward elves?" asked Morty. "How are you going to do that?"
    "I'll find a way," Mickey answered.

That night Mickey and the boys had a great dinner. They finished it up with ice cream and cake. Then Mickey told the boys it was time for bed.

"But it's still early!" cried Morty.

"You need your rest," Mickey told him, "and I have a rush order. It has to be done by morning."

    The boys went off to bed. Before they crawled under the covers, they set their alarm clock for midnight.

    When the boys were asleep, Mickey got busy. He took out and wrapped the two bikes Morty and Ferdie had liked best. He tied the packages with big bows. He put them down beside the worktable. Then he began to fix a bike.

    Soon his eyes were closed.

It was very late when Morty and Ferdie peeked out of the back of the shop. They saw Mickey at his workbench.

"Sound asleep, like he usually is," whispered Morty.

"Where would he be without those elves?" asked Ferdie.

The boys tiptoed to the worktable. They looked for a bike that needed fixing. There was none. Instead there were two big packages tied up with bows.

"To Morty," said a tag on one package.

"To Ferdie," said a tag on the second package.

The boys untied the bows and folded back the paper. And what did they see? They saw the two bikes they wanted. Mickey hadn't sold them after all. He had only gift-wrapped them!

"Thanks!" said the note on one bike. "Without you elves, Mickey's Bike Shop would have closed weeks ago."

The next day, Mickey and the boys took a holiday. They went riding on their bikes—all three of them. Mickey had picked out a brand new bike for himself, too.

"You're a great uncle," said Morty as they sped
along.

"And you're great nephews," said Mickey. "The
bikes are the least I could do for you to thank you
for all your help."

"Aw, it was nothing, Uncle Mickey," Morty said.

"After all," Ferdie said, "that's what families are
for!"

Think About It

Mickey's Mixed-Up Letter

Below is a letter that Mickey wrote to Minnie, telling her all about his opening day in the bike shop. But, he's gotten some of his facts mixed up. Can you pick out the two sentences that are wrong in Mickey's letter?

Dear Minnie,

Today we opened my new bike shop. We had many customers from the very first moment we opened.

Morty and Ferdie were a very big help. They are very good nephews. We were so busy today that we never even got a chance to sit down.

Talk to you soon.

Love,
Mickey

After your child does the activities in this book, refer to the *Young Readers Guide* for the answers to these activities and for additional games, activities, and ideas.

Do You Remember. . .?

See how many of the details below you remember from the story.

1. How many customers came into Mickey's Bike Shop the first day?

2. Why did the first customer need his bike fixed by the next day?

3. How many nights did Morty and Ferdie wake up in the middle of the night to fix a bicycle?

4. How did Mickey figure out that it was Morty and Ferdie who were fixing the bikes, not elves?

5. What did Mickey do at the end of the story to show Morty and Ferdie how grateful he was for their help?

Fun With Words

Bicycle Word Search

In the word-search puzzle below, find the four bicycle words given in the Clue Box. (Hint: Words may be found from left to right and top to bottom.)

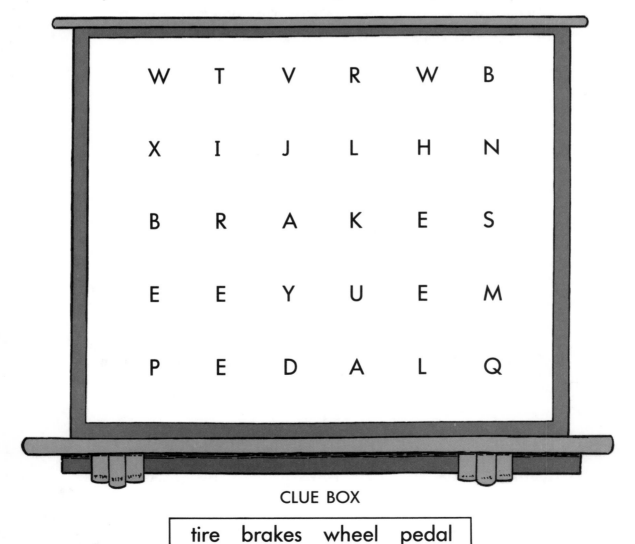

```
W   T   V   R   W   B
X   I   J   L   H   N
B   R   A   K   E   S
E   E   Y   U   E   M
P   E   D   A   L   Q
```

CLUE BOX

tire   brakes   wheel   pedal

Bicycle Mix-Up

In Mickey's Bike Shop, Mickey wants to sell only things that have to do with riding bicycles. Someone has brought in four things that do not belong in Mickey's shop. Can you point them out?

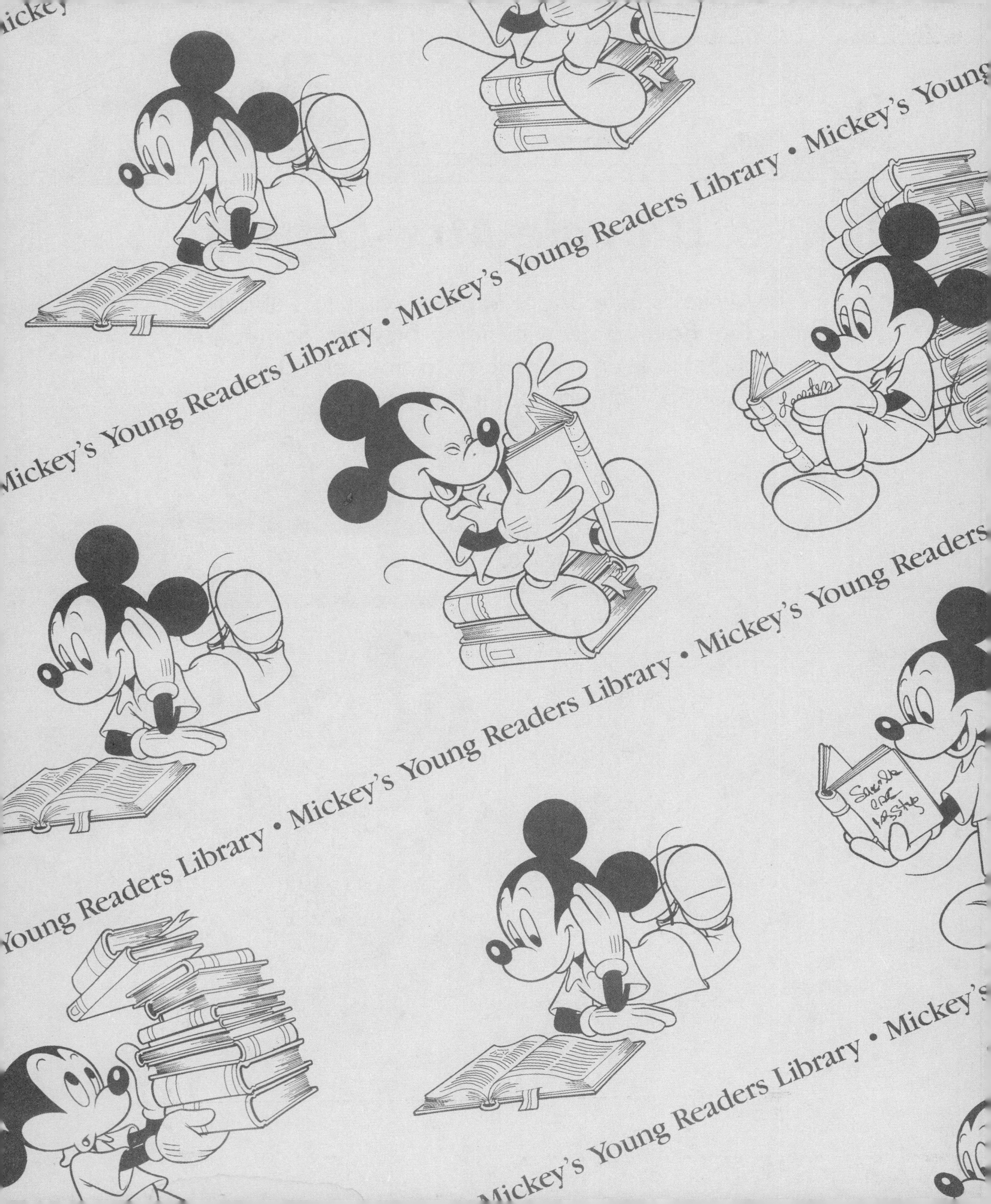